MALSIS BOOKS

FIRST EDITION MAY/5/26

PUBLISHED BY MALSIS BOOKS
CASTLE ROCK, CO

FOR MORE ABOUT THE AUTHORS AND UPCOMING PROJECTS, VISIT: HTTPS://MALSISBOOKS.COM
LIBRARY OF CONGRESS CATALOGING-IN-PUBLICATION DATA:
LCCN 2026907999
ISBN 979-8-9926169-0-3 (PAPERBACK)
ISBN 979-8-9926169-1-0, (EBOOK)

THIS BOOK IS DEDICATED TO:
THOSE WHO SUFFER THE INEVITABLE TRAUMAS THAT RESULT FROM PROTECTING OTHERS, THOSE WHO HELP THEM RECOVER, ESPECIALLY THEIR FAMILIES AND THEIR FAITHFUL SERVICE DOGS, AND ABOVE ALL, THOSE WHO HAVE LOST THEIR LIVES HELPING OTHERS. WE HOPE THIS BOOK CAN TRANSFORM MANY LIVES.

FOREWORD

THERE ARE SOME STORIES YOU READ, AND THEN THERE ARE SOME STORIES YOU FEEL.

THIS IS ONE YOU FEEL.

I HAVE KNOWN JIM FOR A LITTLE WHILE NOW-NOT JUST AS A FRIEND, BUT AS A FELLOW NEW YORKER AND A MAN WHO UNDERSTANDS THE WEIGHT MANY OF US CARRY AFTER A LIFE OF SERVICE. LIKE JIM, I HAVE SPENT YEARS LEARNING HOW TO LIVE WITH EXPERIENCES THAT DON'T SIMPLY FADE WITH TIME. AS A MARINE COMBAT VETERAN WHO HAS STRUGGLED WITH PTSD, I KNOW THAT RECOVERY IS NOT A STRAIGHT LINE. IT IS NOT EASY. AND FOR MANY OF US, IT IS SOMETHING WE CONTINUE TO NAVIGATE EVERY DAY.

THAT'S WHY THIS STORY MATTERS. THIS BOOK SPEAKS TO THE INVISIBLE WOUNDS THAT COME FROM A LIFE SPENT SERVING OTHERS-THE KIND THAT BUILDS OVER TIME AND ARE OFTEN CARRIED IN SILENCE. BUT MORE IMPORTANTLY, IT SPEAKS TO SOMETHING JUST AS REAL: THE POSSIBILITY OF HEALING.

AT IT'S CORE, THIS IS A STORY ABOUT CONNECTION. DOLLY JEANNE IS NOT JUST A COMPANION-SHE REPRESENTS TRUST, PATIENCE, AND THE KIND OF STEADY, UNCONDITIONAL PRESENCE THAT CAN REACH PLACES WORDS CANNOT. IN MANY WAYS, SHE BECOMES A BRIDGE-BETWEEN ISOLATION AND CONNECTION, BETWEEN STRUGGLE AND HEALING.

WHAT MAKES THIS STORY EVEN MORE POWERFUL IS HOW IT WAS TOLD. JIM DIDN'T TELL IT ALONE. HE TOLD IT WITH HIS DAUGHTERS, LYLA AND SHELBY. THERE IS SOMETHING DEEPLY MEANINGFUL ABOUT A FATHER SHARING NOT JUST HIS STRENGTH, BUT HIS VULNERABILITY WITH HIS CHILDREN. IN DOING SO, THIS STORY BECOMES MORE THAN PERSONAL-IT BECOMES A TESTAMENT TO HONESTY, FAMILY, AND THE COURAGE TO BE SEEN AS YOU TRULY ARE.

FOR THOSE WHO HAVE SERVED-WHETHER IN THE MILITARY, LAW ENFORCEMENT, THE FIRE SERVICE, OR ANY ROLE THAT PLACES OTHERS BEFORE YOURSELF-YOU MAY RECOGNIZE PARTS OF YOUR OWN JOURNEY IN THESE PAGES. FOR FAMILIES, THIS BOOK OFFERS A WINDOW INTO BATTLES THAT ARE OFTEN FOUGHT QUIETLY. AND FOR ANYONE WHO HAS EVER FELT LOST OR ALONE, IT IS A REMINDER THAT HEALING IS POSSIBLE-AND THAT IT OFTEN BEGINS WITH CONNECTION.

I HAVE SPENT MANY YEARS IN BOTH THE VETERAN AND RECOVERY COMMUNITIES, AND I HAVE SEEN FIRSTHAND HOW POWERFUL THAT CONNECTION CAN BE. WHETHER IT COMES THROUGH ANOTHER PERSON, A SHARED EXPERIENCE, OR A LOYAL DOG WAITING AT THE DOOR, IT CAN MAKE ALL THE DIFFERENCE.

JIM, LYLA, SHELBY, AND AMANDA-THANK YOU FOR HAVING THE COURAGE TO SHARE THIS STORY.

AND TO THE READER-TAKE YOUR TIME WITH THESE PAGES. YOU MAY FIND MORE THAN JUST A STORY HERE.
YOU MAY FIND A PIECE OF YOURSELF.

KEVIN T. RYAN, SSG, USA, RET.
SGT, USMC (VETERAN)

CHAPTER 1: A LITTER IS BORN
LENNY AND AMBER FINK LIVE IN A RUN DOWN TRAILER. IT'S A RAMSHACKLE MESS! THEY HAVE NO AIR CONDITIONING AND FLIES ARE BUZZING AROUND A SINK FULL OF DIRTY DISHES.
YOU BETTER GET A JOB LENNY! AND FIX THAT DOOR. THESE FLIES ARE EATING ME ALIVE!
YEAH, YEAH, YEAH. QUIT NAGGING ME, AMBER.
ROSE THE MALINOIS DOG IS WHIMPERING, HOWLING, AND BEING IGNORED. LETTING OUT A GROAN, SHE BIRTHS NINE PUPPIES ON A PILE OF DIRTY CLOTHES.
AMBER THROWS A HANDFUL OF DOG FOOD AT HER.
8 WEEKS LATER: THE PUPPIES ESCAPE! ALL NINE PUPPIES TIMIDLY APPROACH AND QUICKLY PUSH PAST THE BROKEN DOOR. THEY SNEAK OUTSIDE WHILE THE FINKS ARE DISTRACTED.
WILL WE EVER FIND SOMEONE TO LOVE US?

BAILEY CURLS UP IN THE SHADE OF A CACTUS AND FALLS ASLEEP. A PRETTY, YOUNG COUNTRY SINGER IN HER EARLY 20'S STEPS OUT OF HER TOUR BUS TO STRETCH, LOOKS DOWN AND SEES BAILEY.
SHE SWOOPS UP THE ADORABLE FURBALL AND RESCUES HER.
ELLA SMELLS A NEIGHBOR COOKING BACON AND DECIDES TO FOLLOW HER NOSE.
SHE WALKS ACROSS THE STREET AND FALLS ASLEEP ON THEIR PORCH IN THE AFTERNOON SUN.
THE PUPPIES, NOW DOWN TO SEVEN, CONTINUE WALKING DOWN THE COUNTRY ROAD TOWARD THE HIGHWAY. LADY STUMBLES DOWN A RIVERBANK WHERE SHE STOPS FOR A DRINK.
A COUPLE SWIMMING SPOTS LADY STRUGGLING. THEY RESCUE THE SPUNKY PUP.
SIX NOW, THEY VENTURE DOWN TO THE HIGHWAY.

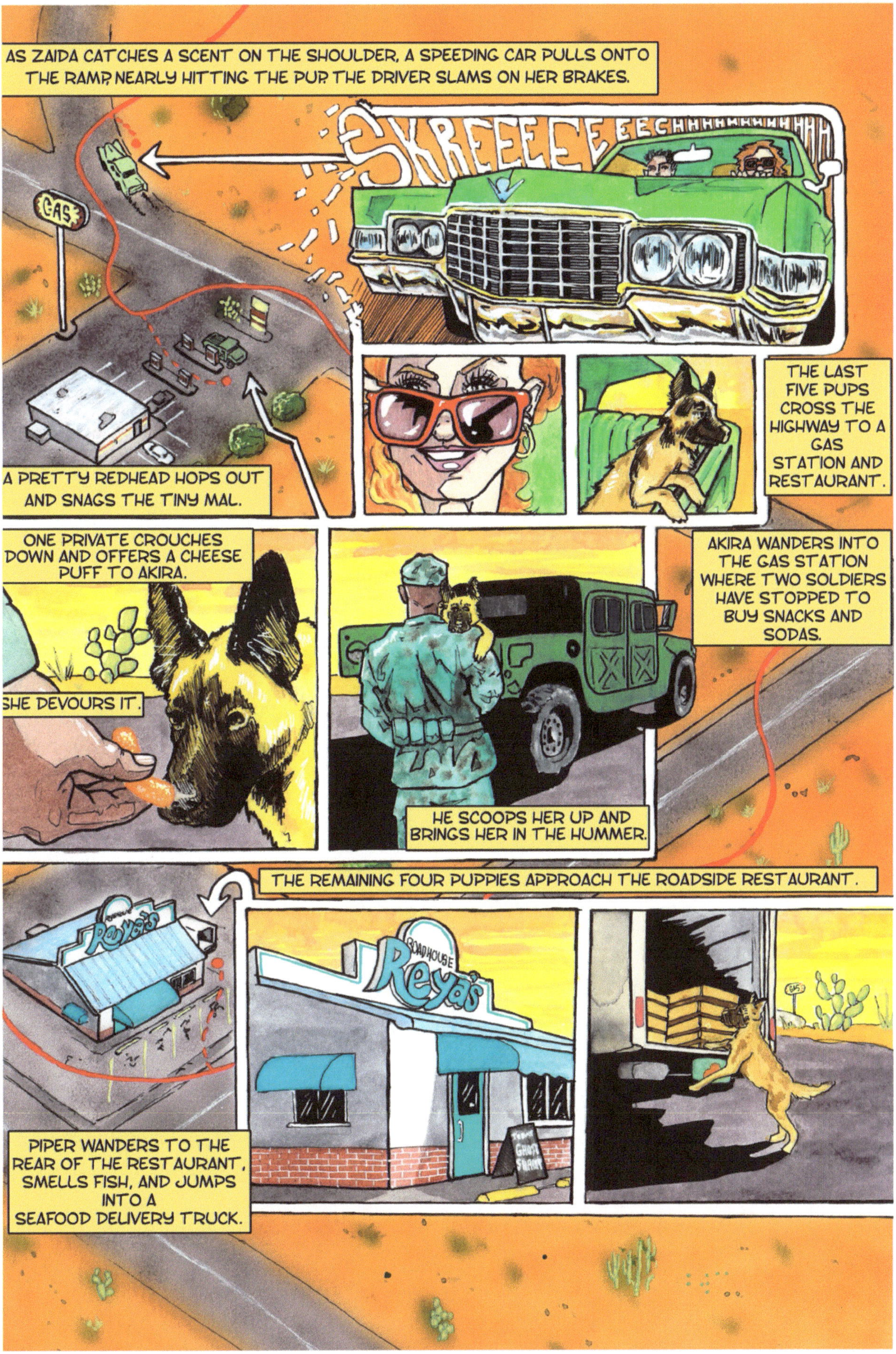
AS ZAIDA CATCHES A SCENT ON THE SHOULDER, A SPEEDING CAR PULLS ONTO THE RAMP, NEARLY HITTING THE PUP. THE DRIVER SLAMS ON HER BRAKES.
SKREEEEEEEECHHHHHHHHHHHH
GAS
A PRETTY REDHEAD HOPS OUT AND SNAGS THE TINY MAL.
THE LAST FIVE PUPS CROSS THE HIGHWAY TO A GAS STATION AND RESTAURANT.
ONE PRIVATE CROUCHES DOWN AND OFFERS A CHEESE PUFF TO AKIRA.
SHE DEVOURS IT.
AKIRA WANDERS INTO THE GAS STATION WHERE TWO SOLDIERS HAVE STOPPED TO BUY SNACKS AND SODAS.
HE SCOOPS HER UP AND BRINGS HER IN THE HUMMER.
THE REMAINING FOUR PUPPIES APPROACH THE ROADSIDE RESTAURANT.
Reya's
ROADHOUSE
Reya's
PIPER WANDERS TO THE REAR OF THE RESTAURANT, SMELLS FISH, AND JUMPS INTO A SEAFOOD DELIVERY TRUCK.

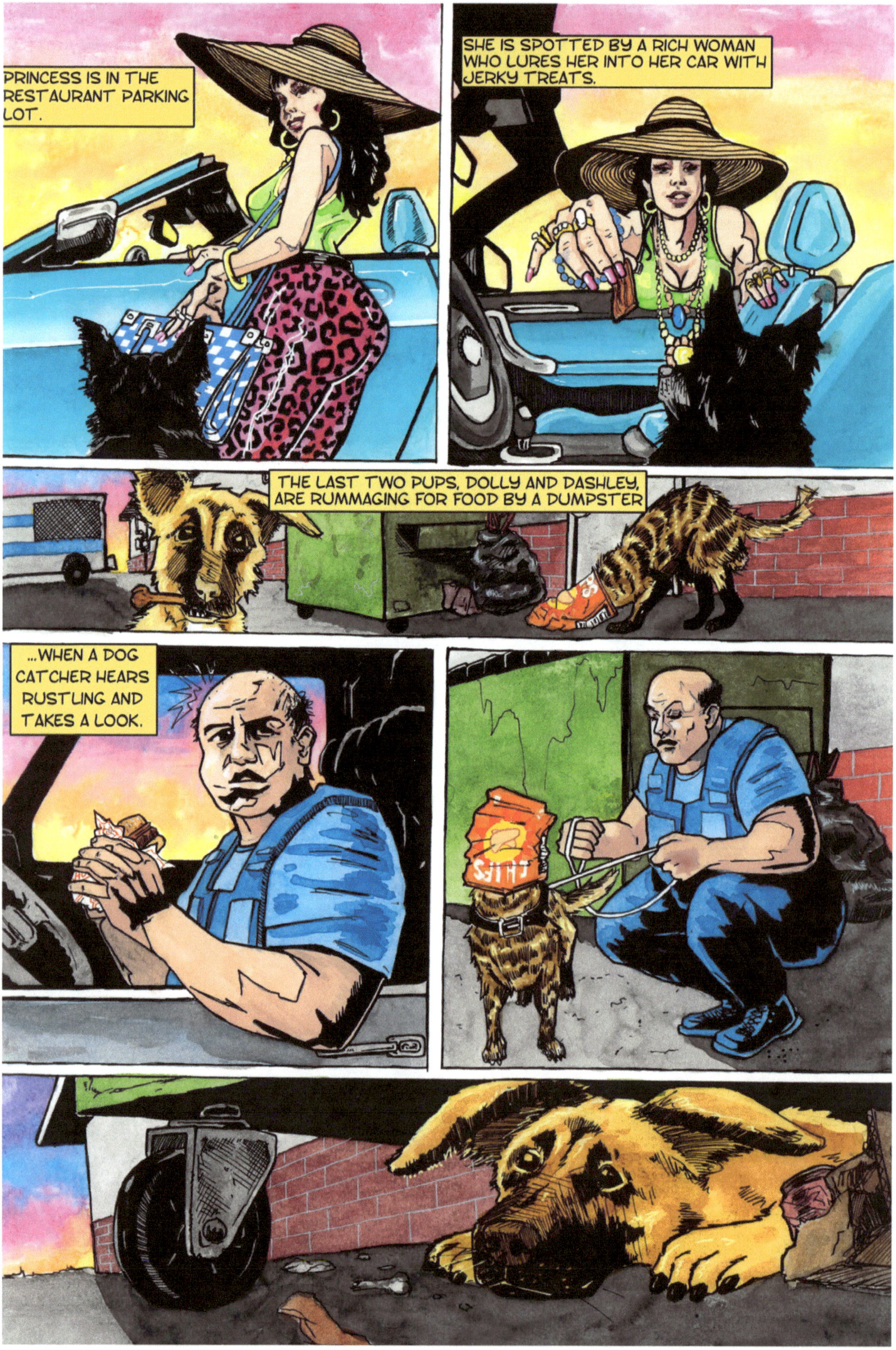
PRINCESS IS IN THE RESTAURANT PARKING LOT.
SHE IS SPOTTED BY A RICH WOMAN WHO LURES HER INTO HER CAR WITH JERKY TREATS.
THE LAST TWO PUPS, DOLLY AND DASHLEY, ARE RUMMAGING FOR FOOD BY A DUMPSTER
...WHEN A DOG CATCHER HEARS RUSTLING AND TAKES A LOOK.
CHIPS

THE VERY LAST PUPPY, DOLLY JEANNE, SCURRIES AWAY THEN SLOWS TO A WALK WHEN SHE REALIZES SHE IS ALL ALONE.
SHOULD I STAY HERE, OR CONTINUE DOWN THE ROAD ALONE? WILL I BE EATEN BY ANIMALS? STARVE OR DIE? SHOULD I GO BACK AND LOOK FOR MY SIBLINGS?

CHAPTER 2: WAY DOWN IN A HOLE
NYC IN THE 1980'S
SMOKE!
14 Street Union Square Station
JULY 1988. TRANSIT POLICE STATIONS, CALLED DISTRICTS, ARE LOCATED IN THE SUBWAY SYSTEM UNDER NYC. JOE WORKS IN MANHATTAN IN A SUBWAY STATION THAT IS HOT, NOISY, AND CROWDED.
ROLL CALL AT DISTRICT 44 UNION SQUARE
I ♥ NY
Ya Mama's Favorite
DOUGHNUT
R
Queens Blvd
Broadway
2476

THIS IS JOSEPH FLANNERY. HE'S ONLY BEEN ON THE FORCE A SHORT TIME NOW. MANY TRANSIT POLICE OFFICERS WORK PATROL ALONE.
JOE OBSERVES THE K9S IN ACTION WITH AWE AND ADMIRATION.
Western Electric
HE LOVES THEM! HE EVEN CONSIDERS GETTING A SHEPHERD OF HIS OWN.
NO ENT

CRIME WAS HIGH IN THE 1980S.
TOLKENS 1.15
SERVICE CHANGES
frankie
SAMO

Sob
STORY-
SOMETIMES JOE AND HIS FRIENDS DRINK TO TAKE THE EDGE OFF OF THEIR STRESSFUL WORK LIFE.
DISTRICT 44
JOE HAS BEEN TO MANY TRAGIC "LINE OF DUTY" FUNERALS FOR HIS BROTHER AND SISTER POLICE OFFICERS. EACH ONE REMINDS HIM OF THE RISK ALL COPS TAKE ON A DAILY BASIS.

JOE HAS HAD MANY LIFE-THREATENING EXPERIENCES WHILE IN THE POLICE DEPARTMENT. SOME OF THESE CAUSE FLASHBACKS, NIGHTMARES, AND ANXIETY. THE STRESS BECOMES OVERWHELMING, AFFECTING EVERY PART OF HIS LIFE.
JOE TURNS IN HIS BADGE, ENDING HIS POLICE CAREER.
SOON AFTER, HE TALKS ON THE PHONE WITH A RETIRED COP BUDDY, FRANK G. HE TELLS JOE WHAT LIFE IS LIKE IN RETIREMENT.
Y'KNOW, WHENEVER I HEAR A LOUD NOISE OR WHEN SOMEBODY IS BEHIND ME, I FEEL LIKE I'M BACK IN THE SUBWAY AT WEST 4TH AND WAVERLY ABOUT TO BE STABBED IN THE BACK AGAIN. I'M CONSTANTLY LOOKING OVER MY SHOULDER. DOC SAYS I HAVE POST TRAUMATIC STRESS DISORDER, BUT I DON'T THINK SO.
DO YOU THINK YOU CAN EVER RECOVER FROM PTSD, IF YOU DO HAVE IT?
I'M NOT SURE, BUD.
FLANNERY
5494

CHAPTER 3: K9 TRAINING IS RUFF
BEWARE OF DOG
NO TRESPASSING
PRIVATE PROPERTY
"MAD DOGS" K9 ACADEMY
WANDERING DOWN A COUNTRY ROAD, DOLLY HEARS BARKING AND INVESTIGATES.
AFTER SQUEEZING THROUGH THE FENCE, SHE IS FOUND BY MATTHEW "MATTY MAD DOGS" MCKOY. HE RECOGNIZES THAT SHE IS A MALINOIS PUP AND DECIDES TO KEEP AND TRAIN HER.

MATTY IS A DECORATED VETERAN.
K9 ACADEMY
USMC
ATTACK ON AMERICA
ALWAYS A PATRIOT, HE DECIDED TO ENLIST AFTER THE TERROR ATTACKS ON SEPTEMBER 11TH, 2001. HE SERVED ALONGSIDE K9S IN IRAQ AND AFGHANISTAN.

MATTY REMEMBERS HIS LAST TOUR OF DUTY THAT LEFT HIM TRAUMATIZED. HIS HUMVEE WAS AMBUSHED AND BLOWN UP BY AN IED. HE LOST HIS LEG AND IS NOW A BELOW THE KNEE AMPUTEE.

FORMERLY AN OUTGOING GUY, HE SUFFERS FROM COMBAT-RELATED TRAUMA AND IS MORE COMFORTABLE AROUND DOGS THAN PEOPLE.
HE SLEEPS WITH HIS PACK OF MALINOIS DOGS BECAUSE THEY MAKE HIM FEEL SAFE, ESPECIALLY WHEN HE IS SHOCKED AWAKE BY A FRIGHTENING NIGHTMARE.
THE VA DIAGNOSED HIM WITH PTSD BUT HE DOESN'T TAKE HIS MEDICATION.

DOLLY IS SMART AND BONDS WITH MATTY.
SHE LEARNS SKILLS TO HELP SUPPORT PEOPLE
DOLLY WATCHES THE OTHER DOGS TRAIN.
SHE'S INSPIRED, BUT SCARED.
THE SCHOOL IS LOUD AND WILD. THERE IS A LOT OF FEROCIOUS BARKING.
DOLLY GETS EVEN MORE NERVOUS AND SHUTS DOWN. HIDING IN HER CRATE, SHE IS ALONE AND NO LONGER USEFUL TO ANYONE.

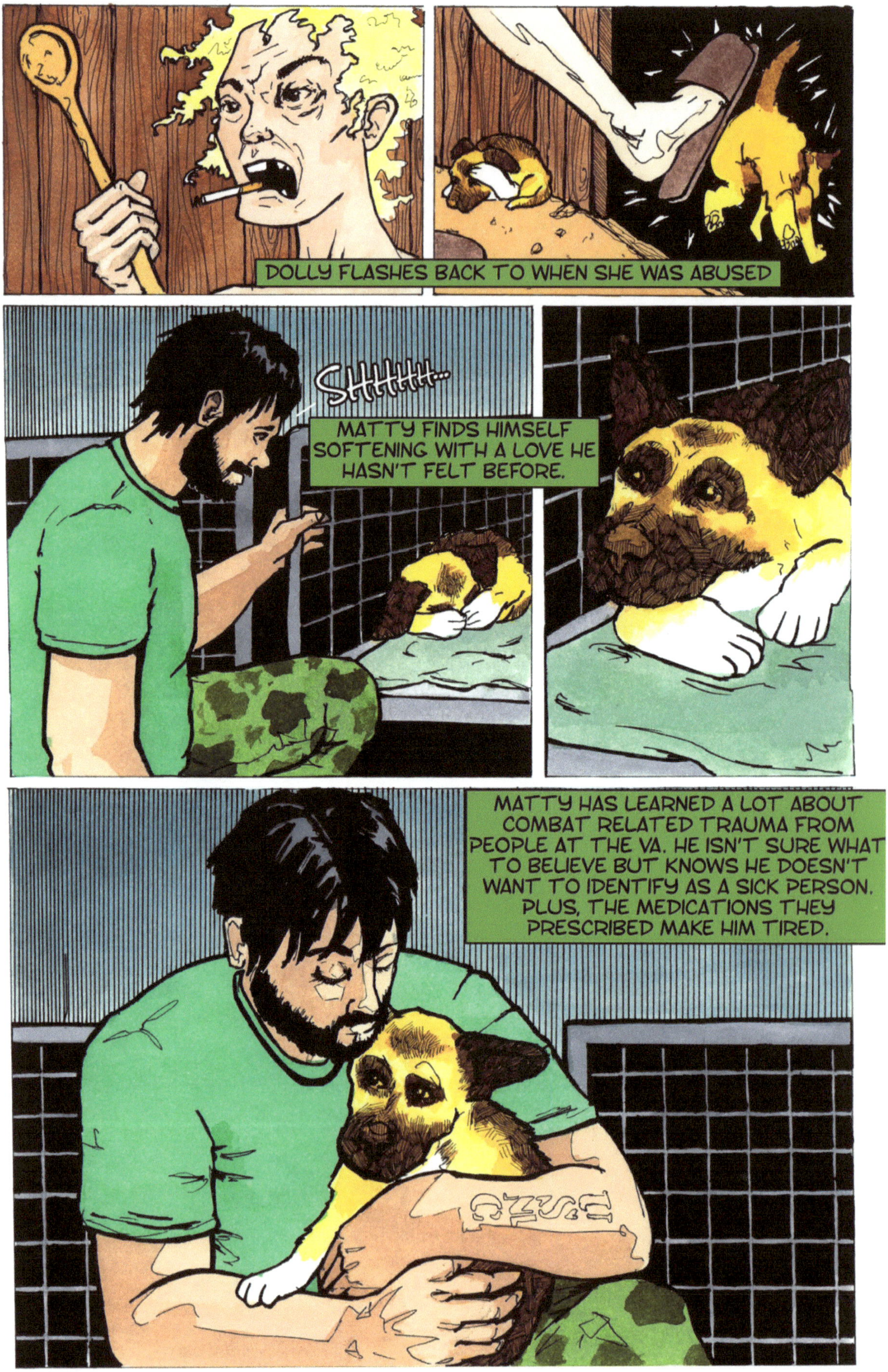
DOLLY FLASHES BACK TO WHEN SHE WAS ABUSED
SHHHHH...
MATTY FINDS HIMSELF SOFTENING WITH A LOVE HE HASN'T FELT BEFORE.
MATTY HAS LEARNED A LOT ABOUT COMBAT RELATED TRAUMA FROM PEOPLE AT THE VA. HE ISN'T SURE WHAT TO BELIEVE BUT KNOWS HE DOESN'T WANT TO IDENTIFY AS A SICK PERSON. PLUS, THE MEDICATIONS THEY PRESCRIBED MAKE HIM TIRED.
USMC

CHAPTER 4: WELCOME TO THE HOUSE OF PAIN
FDNY ACADEMY
AFTER LEAVING THE TRANSIT POLICE, JOE IS HIRED BY THE FDNY AND IS SWORN IN.
JOE TRAINS FOR 8 WEEKS.
HE'S ASSIGNED TO ENGINE 277 AND THEN LADDER 112 IN BUSHWICK, BROOKLYN.
112
FDNY
FIREFIGHTERS IN NEW YORK CITY RESPOND TO ALL TYPES OF FIRES AND EMERGENCIES.

FIREMEN TAKE ON STRESS EVERY DAY. EVEN SO-CALLED ROUTINE RUNS WORSEN TRAUMA OVER TIME.
MY BABIES ARE IN THERE!!!
NO FRILLS
112
277
277

JOE FLANNERY IS IN BROOKLYN ON THE ROOF OF A ROW FRAME BUILDING
JOE AND MANY OTHERS WORKED TIRELESS SHIFTS AT THE WORLD TRADE CENTER SITE, SIFTING THROUGH RUBBLE, ATTEMPTING TO FIND THE REMAINS OF THE LOST.
PAPD
NYPD

JOE LOVES THE WORK, ENJOYS SERVING THE PUBLIC, BUT EVERY TIME ONE OF HIS FELLOW FIREFIGHTERS DIES, IT LEAVES A MARK.
JOE NOTICES THAT HE IS SOMETIMES UPTIGHT, OFTEN WHEN HE'S NOT WORKING.
JOE HAS RECURRING NIGHTMARES. HE WAKES UP ANXIOUS AND CANNOT FALL BACK TO SLEEP.
OCTOBER 20
25 YEARS!
RETIRE!!!
JOE TURNS IN HIS BADGE, RETIRES, AND PLANS ON RELAXING A LITTLE IN HIS HOME BY THE OCEAN.

ALERT
HURRICANE SANDY
PATH OF DESTRUCTION
HURRICANE WINDS EXPECTED TO REACH SPEEDS OF 115MPH
SUPERSTORM SANDY WARNING
PEOPLE ADVISED TO:
- EVACUATE DANGER ZONE
- FILL TUBS OF WATER
NY5
HURRICANE SANDY STRIKES.
JOE, UNDER STRESS, WATCHES HIS HOUSE FLOOD DURING THE HURRICANE.
DISTRESSED BY THE DEVASTATION OF HIS BEACH TOWN, JOE AND HIS WIFE MINDY, DECIDE TO MOVE.

CHAPTER 5: SAY HELLO TO MY LITTLE FRIENDS
MATTY "MAD DOG" MCKOY'S ACADEMY
HEY
WHOA!!
YOU CAN'T JUST BARGE IN LIKE THAT! YOU KNOW HOW I AM.
SORRY. ANOTHER BAD NIGHT OF SLEEP?
YEAH. THAT ONE NIGHT-MARE. IT JUST WON'T GO AWAY!

DOLLY CATCHES JILLIAN'S EYE ON THE WAY OUT.
RUFF!
JILLIAN INQUIRES ABOUT THE SAD PUP.
WHAT'S WRONG WITH HER?
SHE'S A GOOD GIRL BUT SHE'S TOO GENTLE FOR OUR KIND OF K9 TRAINING.
MATTY AGREES THAT DOLLY SHOULD GO WITH JILLIAN.
SIGH
COULD THIS BE SOMEONE TO LOVE?
DOLLY MEETS HER NEW FRIENDS.

KING
ATHENA
SNAKE
GERMY
CHI CHI
DOLLY HASN'T FIT IN YET.
DINNER!

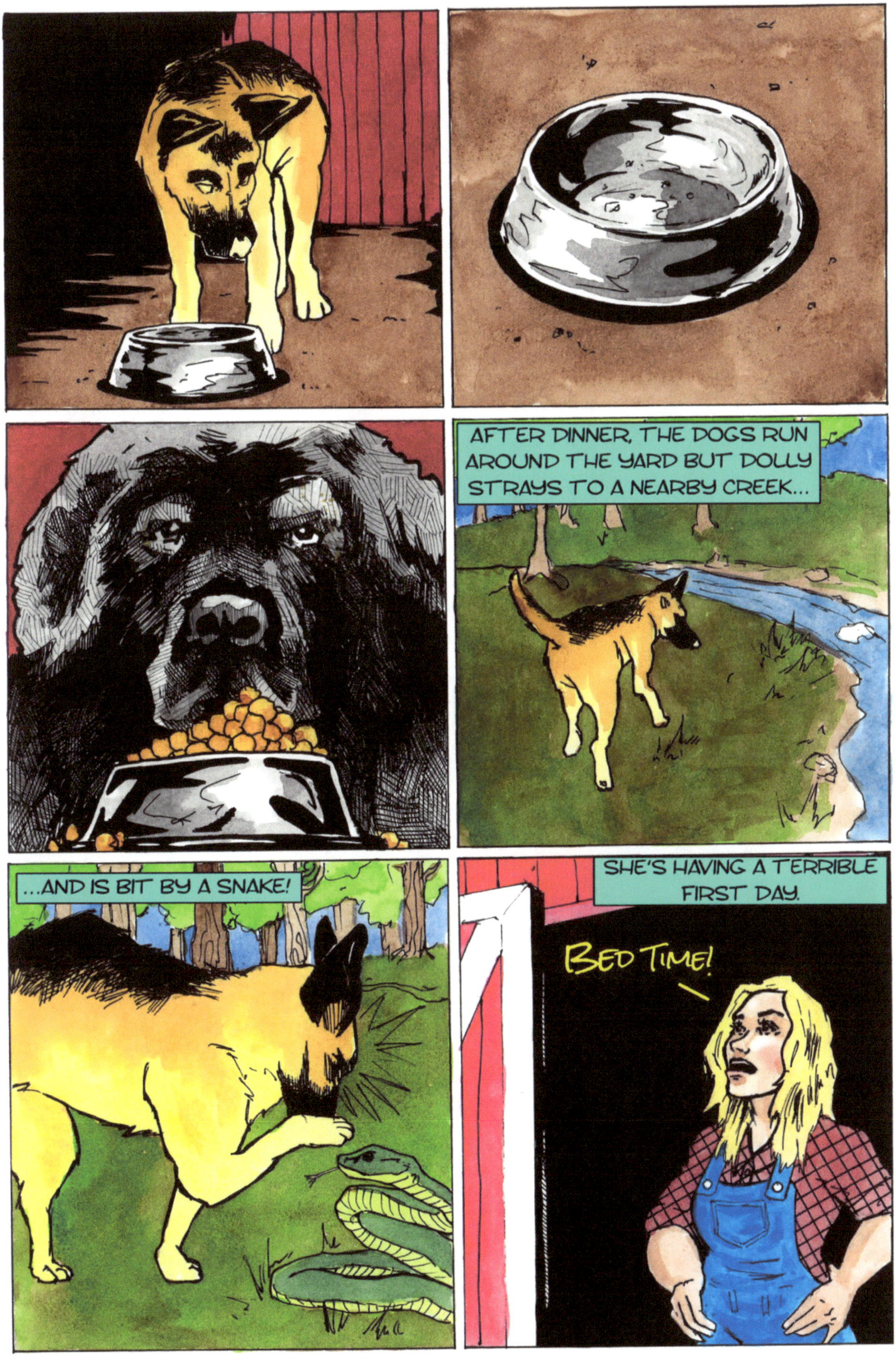
AFTER DINNER, THE DOGS RUN AROUND THE YARD BUT DOLLY STRAYS TO A NEARBY CREEK...
...AND IS BIT BY A SNAKE!
SHE'S HAVING A TERRIBLE FIRST DAY.
BED TIME!

THE DOGS SETTLE IN FOR THE NIGHT.
WHEN DOLLY FINDS HER SPOT, ALL HER HAY IS GONE.
PSST, PSST. WAKE UP.
GERMY SHARES WITH DOLLY.
COULD THERE BE HOPE FOR ME?

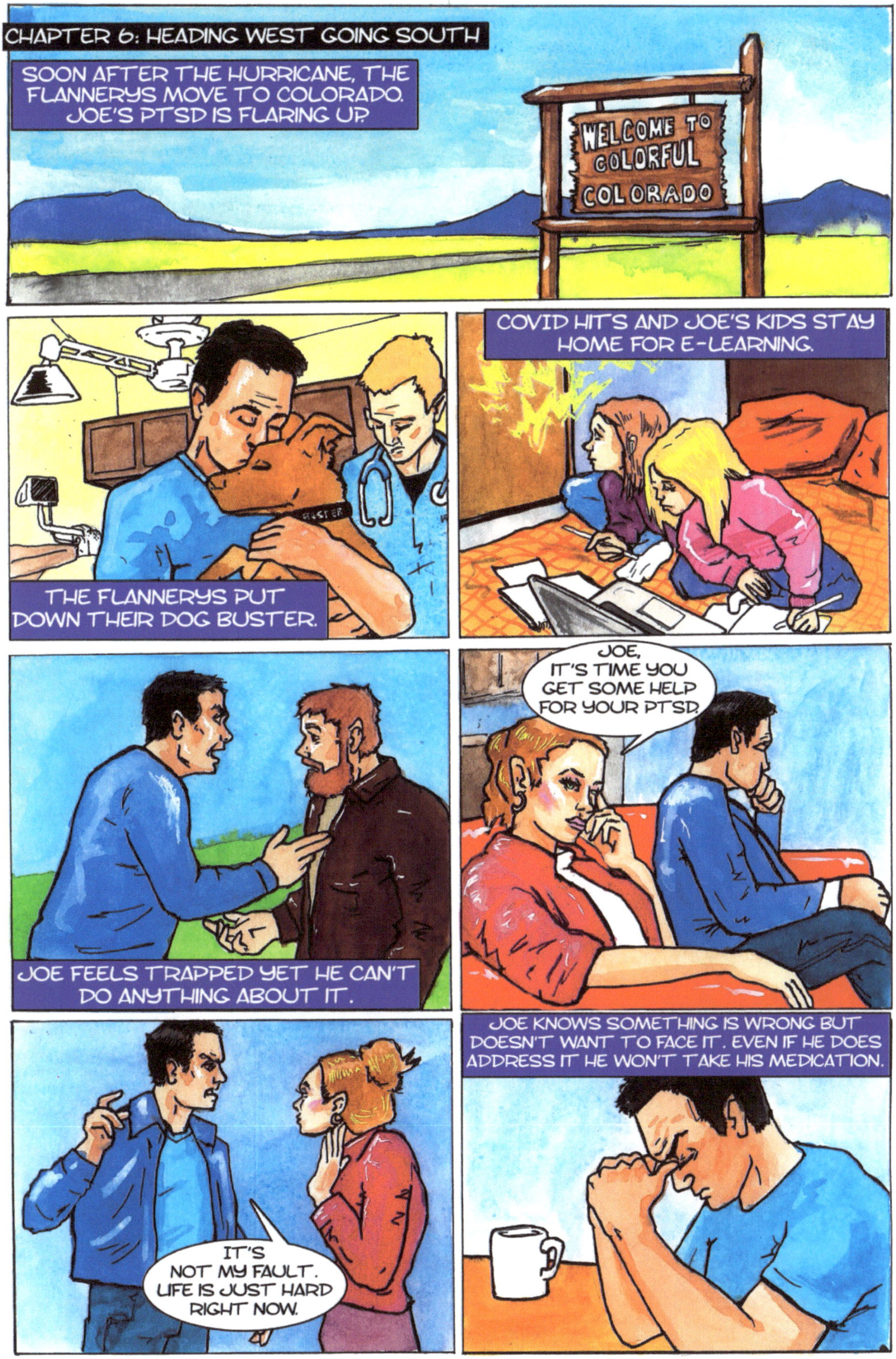
CHAPTER 6: HEADING WEST GOING SOUTH
SOON AFTER THE HURRICANE, THE FLANNERYS MOVE TO COLORADO. JOE'S PTSD IS FLARING UP.
WELCOME TO COLORFUL COLORADO
BUSTER
THE FLANNERYS PUT DOWN THEIR DOG BUSTER.
COVID HITS AND JOE'S KIDS STAY HOME FOR E-LEARNING.
JOE FEELS TRAPPED YET HE CAN'T DO ANYTHING ABOUT IT.
JOE, IT'S TIME YOU GET SOME HELP FOR YOUR PTSD.
IT'S NOT MY FAULT. LIFE IS JUST HARD RIGHT NOW.
JOE KNOWS SOMETHING IS WRONG BUT DOESN'T WANT TO FACE IT. EVEN IF HE DOES ADDRESS IT HE WON'T TAKE HIS MEDICATION.

CHAPTER 7: WISH UPON A STAR
MEANWHILE, BACK AT THE RANCH...
YOU'D BETTER NOT EAT YOUR FOOD TONIGHT
WHAT'S WRONG?
EVERYTHING.
ATHENA WILL HELP YOU, TALK TO HER.
DON'T LOSE HOPE, FOR YOU WILL KNOW WHEN YOU FEEL LOVE.

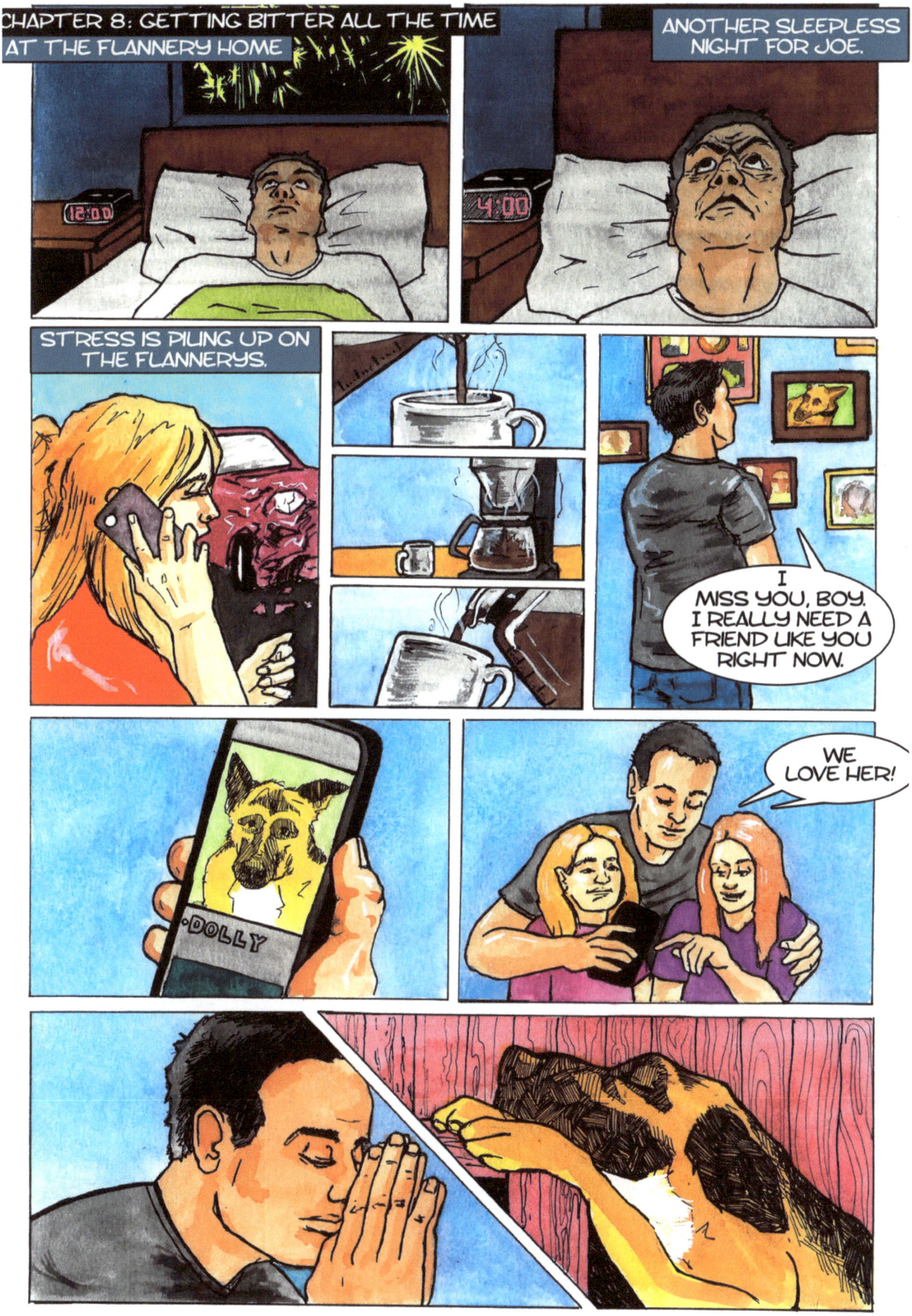
CHAPTER 8: GETTING BITTER ALL THE TIME
AT THE FLANNERY HOME
12:00
ANOTHER SLEEPLESS NIGHT FOR JOE.
4:00
STRESS IS PILING UP ON THE FLANNERYS.
I MISS YOU, BOY. I REALLY NEED A FRIEND LIKE YOU RIGHT NOW.
DOLLY
WE LOVE HER!

CHAPTER 9: PHONE CALLS AND FIREBALLS
HELLO, JILLIAN? I'M INTERESTED IN THE SHEPHERD MIX, DOLLY. MY KIDS ARE LITTLE, SO I NEED A CALM DOG.
THAT DOG IS HALF BELGIAN MALINOIS, A VERY ACTIVE BREED. SHE IS CALM BUT MAY GET WILD SOON.
OH, I DON'T THINK SHE'S RIGHT FOR US. THANK YOU.
ONE WEEK LATER LIGHTNING STRIKES WINGER, NEW MEXICO. THE DIAMOND J HAS NO POWER!
BOOM
CRACK!
MEANWHILE, JILLIAN IS ON A PHONE CALL WITH THE LOCAL VET, DOCTOR MITCHELL. THE DIAMOND J IS FAILING AND SHE WON'T BE ABLE TO KEEP THE DOGS MUCH LONGER.
DOLLY ISN'T DOING WELL. SHE'S NOT ADJUSTING TO THE PACK AND NOBODY WANTS HER. I'M NOT SURE WHAT TO DO, BUT I KNOW I CAN'T AFFORD TO FEED ALL THESE DOGS. THE RANCH IS OUT OF LUCK. I MIGHT NEED TO MOVE TO TOWN.
ZAP!
WHAT?
WHAT MITCHELL HEARD THROUGH THE PHONE WAS A GARBLED, TERRIBLE MESS.

CHAPTER 10: THE DECISION
AT THE SAME TIME....
ANIMAL ADOPT
I DON'T KNOW IF WE ARE READY FOR A NEW PUP. WE ARE STILL GRIEVING BUSTER.
I THINK WE CAN LEARN TO LOVE A NEW DOG. I'M GOING TO NEW MEXICO TO MEET DOLLY.
TRAFFIC! UGHHHH!
I HATE TRAFFIC!
JOE HAS BEEN ON THE HIGHWAY FOR AN HOUR! HE'S BLOCKED BY A GREEN CHILE SPILL. JOE, DAYDREAMING ABOUT DOLLY, IS DETERMINED TO GET TO WINGER.
PET CREMATORIUM
TONYS
PIZZA · PASTA · SEA
TODAY'S SPECIAL BROCCOLINI + GARLIC KNOTS!
HEY ANGELS, IT'S MITCH, WE NEED YOU TO BRING THE TRUCK TO THE DIAMOND J.
YEAH, SURE, I'M ON IT.
TONY'S

CHAPTER 11: LET'S ROLL
DOLLY IS IN TROUBLE!
LET'S ROLL!
WHAT IF IT WAS YOU?
I'M NOT GONNA WASTE MY TIME.
DOLLY IS OUR FRIEND. WE NEED TO SAVE HER.
DOLLY HASN'T FELT LOVE AND MAYBE NEVER WILL. SHE WON'T GIVE UP.
JOE ARRIVES AT THE RANCH.
I KNOW I'M LOVABLE.

IT'S NOT OVER YET!
SMASH!

SHE'S THE ONE!
REALLY?
YES!
WHAT JUST HAPPENED? WHY IS TONY HERE?
I'M SORRY MA'AM, I WAS JUST FOLLOWING ORDERS.
YEAH, YOU TOLD ME ON THE PHONE 'CALL THE KILL TRUCK, WE NEED TO PUT HER DOWN.'
I SAID; 'THE RANCH IS OUT OF LUCK; WE MIGHT NEED TO MOVE TO TOWN.'
I'M JUST GLAD I GET TO TAKE HER HOME!

BACK AT HOME, JOE'S FAMILY WAITS FOR DOLLY, THEY ARE EXCITED TO MEET THEIR NEW PUP!

CHAPTER 12: RISE LIKE A PHOENIX
SHE'S FURRY AND OH SO CUTE!
DOLLY HIDES IN THE LAUNDRY BUT SOON COMES AROUND
DOLLY BEGINS TO WARM UP TO THE FLANNERYS. SHE OFFERS JOE EMOTIONAL SUPPORT AND NEVER LEAVES HIS SIDE.
SHE HAS TRAUMA FROM HER ROUGH LIFE AND SOON, DOLLY STARTS TO TRUST THE WHOLE FAMILY.

CHAPTER 13: THE FIRE AND THE FURRY
DOLLY HEARS SCREAMING AND GLASS BREAKING.
THE NEIGHBORS ARE TRAPPED BY FIRE.
HELP!
JOE IS LOCKED IN A TRANCE THINKING BACK TO A 747 CRASHING INTO A NURSING HOME IN BROOKLYN.
DOLLY JUMPS UP TO BRING JOE BACK TO REALITY.
DOLLY NOOOOOO!!!

JOE IS PUSHED DOWN BY THE SMOKE AND HEAT.
JOE FOLLOWS DOLLY.
BARK!!!!!...
JOE STARTS TO GRAB THE WIFE WHEN THE CEILING COLLAPSES TRAPPING THEM BOTH.

DOLLY IS ON FIRE!
THE FIREMEN ARRIVE.
DOLLY PUTS HER FLAMING FUR OUT IN THE SNOW.
PSSSHHH
OOOWWWOOO!!!...
DOLLY GRABS THE FIREMEN AND LEADS THEM TO JOE
JOE'S OTHER NEIGHBOR, NICK BEAGLES, RESCUES THE HUSBAND.

WILD WHAT ONE CANDLE CAN DO!
THE FIREMEN FIND JOE AND BRING HIM TO THE EMERGENCY ROOM.
MINDY TAKES DOLLY TO THE ANIMAL HOSPITAL.
A DOCTOR SPEAKS WITH JOE ABOUT HIS REACTION AT THE FIRE
SHE SUGGESTS JOE MAY BE SUFFERING FROM PTSD.
HE FINALLY ADMITS HE HAS A PROBLEM.

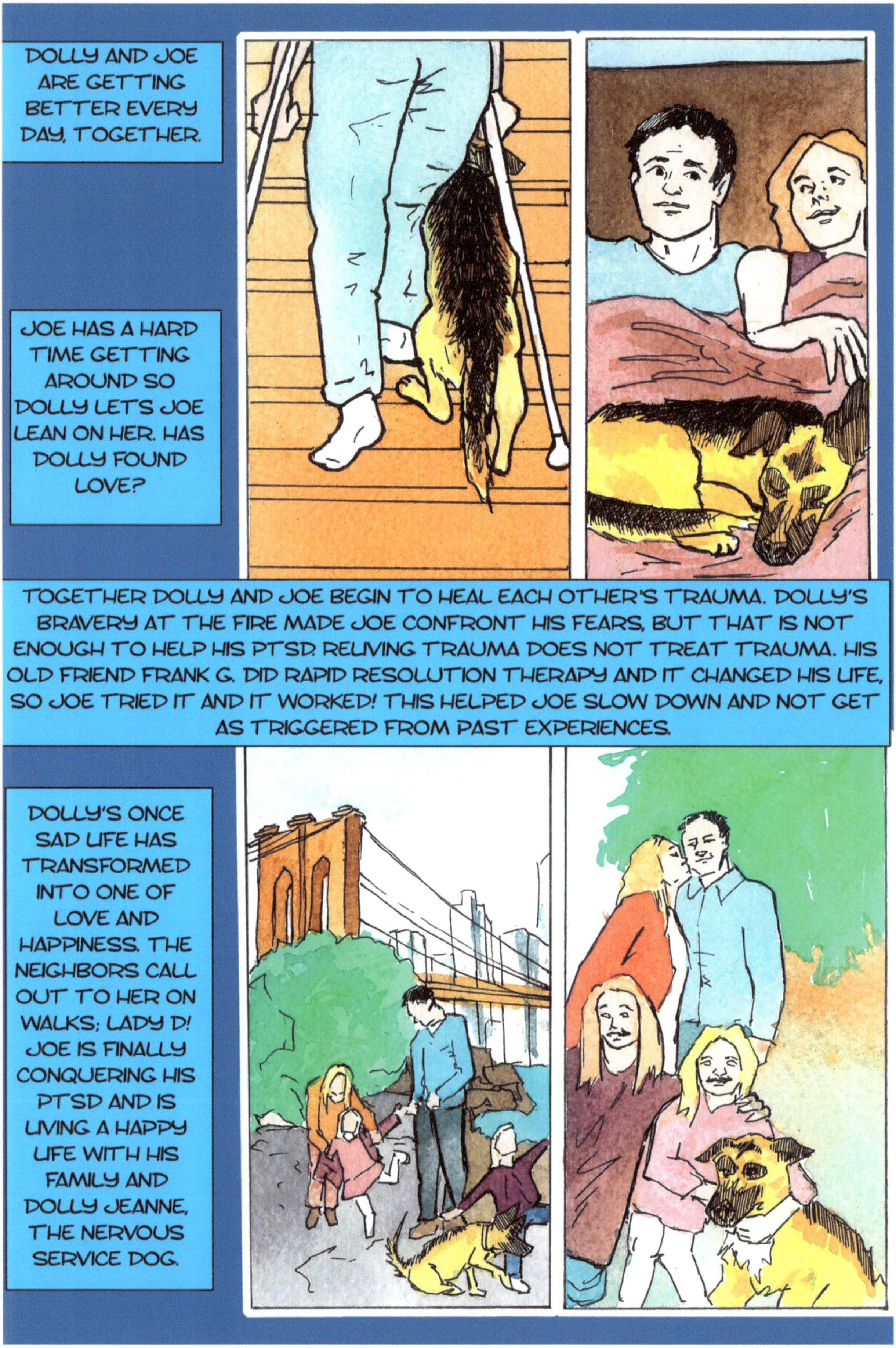
DOLLY AND JOE ARE GETTING BETTER EVERY DAY, TOGETHER.
JOE HAS A HARD TIME GETTING AROUND SO DOLLY LET'S JOE LEAN ON HER. HAS DOLLY FOUND LOVE?
TOGETHER DOLLY AND JOE BEGIN TO HEAL EACH OTHER'S TRAUMA. DOLLY'S BRAVERY AT THE FIRE MADE JOE CONFRONT HIS FEARS, BUT THAT IS NOT ENOUGH TO HELP HIS PTSD. RELIVING TRAUMA DOES NOT TREAT TRAUMA. HIS OLD FRIEND FRANK G. DID RAPID RESOLUTION THERAPY AND IT CHANGED HIS LIFE, SO JOE TRIED IT AND IT WORKED! THIS HELPED JOE SLOW DOWN AND NOT GET AS TRIGGERED FROM PAST EXPERIENCES.
DOLLY'S ONCE SAD LIFE HAS TRANSFORMED INTO ONE OF LOVE AND HAPPINESS. THE NEIGHBORS CALL OUT TO HER ON WALKS; LADY D! JOE IS FINALLY CONQUERING HIS PTSD AND IS LIVING A HAPPY LIFE WITH HIS FAMILY AND DOLLY JEANNE, THE NERVOUS SERVICE DOG.

VA CLINIC
EPILOGUE: THE RECKONING:
MATTY'S INSIDE JOB.
EVERY DOG HAS IT'S DAY
PTSD
A DOCTOR ASKS WHAT INSPIRED HIM TO FINALLY ACCEPT HELP?
MATTY THINKS BACK TO HIS TIME WITH DOLLY.
PTSD
THERE WAS ONE SPECIAL DOG IN MY LIFE WHO SHOWED ME THAT HEALING WAS POSSIBLE.
MATTY LEAVES THE VA WITH A TREATMENT PLAN.
VA CLINIC
JILLIAN SURPRISES MATTY WITH A SERVICE DOG PUP OF HIS OWN

EARLY PRAISE FOR DOLLY JEANNE

"AS A RETIRED FIRST RESPONDER WHO HAS DEALT WITH PTSD IN THE PAST, DOLLY JEANNE IS A GREAT REMINDER OF HOW IMPORTANT IT IS TO CONNECT WITH SOMEONE TO HELP YOU GET THROUGH YOUR DARK MOMENTS EVEN IF THAT CONNECTION IS WITH A DOG. IT CERTAINLY BROUGHT BACK A LOT OF MEMORIES OF WHAT I SAW AS A FIREFIGHTER AND EMT AND HOW GRATEFUL I WAS THAT I SOUGHT COUNSELING FOR MY PTSD WHEN I DID. I LOVED THE ARTWORK WHICH REALLY CAPTURED THE DARK AND HAPPY MOMENTS OVER THE YEARS. MY 12 YEAR OLD LOVED READING IT AND IF WE DIDN'T HAVE A DOG ALREADY SHE WOULD HAVE DEFINITELY MADE US GET ONE AFTER READING THIS."."
- CARLOS LIRIANO, FDNY LIEUTENANT (RET.)

"THIS BOOK SERVES AS A BEAUTIFUL AND HOPEFUL EXAMPLE OF HOW A FAMILY, UNITED THROUGH THE DEPTHS AND COMPLEXITIES OF PTSD, CAN TRANSFORM TRAUMA PATTERNS USING THE POWER OF CONNECTION AND THE CREATIVE SPIRIT. SHELBY AND LYLA INSPIRE A DEEP CALL TO COURAGE, THAT IS, TO HONOR THE CREATIVE SPARK WITHIN."
- DR. DANIELLE ALEXANDER, DPT, M.A., PH.D(C), SOMATIC EXPERIENCING PRACTITIONER®

"DOLLY JEANNE IS A POWERFUL REMINDER THAT THOSE WHO DEVOTE THEIR LIVES TO HELPING OTHERS OFTEN DO SO AT GREAT PERSONAL COST, CARRYING UNSEEN BURDENS THAT MAY GROW HEAVIER WITH TIME. YET EVEN IN LIFE'S DARKEST MOMENTS, THE NERVOUS SERVICE DOG SHOWS US THAT HELP CAN COME FROM THE MOST UNEXPECTED PLACES. AS PATHS INTERTWINE AND HOPE FEELS DISTANT, IT IS AN UNLIKELY FRIENDSHIP AND THE POWER OF CONNECTION THAT BECOMES A GUIDING LIGHT."
- RICK ALEXANDER, FORMER SPECIAL OPERATIONS COMBAT MEDIC

"DOLLY JEANNE THE NERVOUS SERVICE DOG" IS A SWEET AND POWERFUL STORY OF RESILIENCE AND HOPE. IT DEMONSTRATES HOW PAIN AND TRAUMA CAN ENDURE AND HOW WITH LOVE, SUPPORT, THE POWER OF FRIENDSHIP & FAMILY AND OUR INCREDIBLE ANIMALS IT IS POSSIBLE TO FIND A WAY FORWARD. MANY OF THE TREATMENTS DON'T GET YOU WHERE YOU'RE LOOKING TO GO AND GETTING THE RIGHT HELP AT THE RIGHT TIME CAN BE TRULY TRANSFORMATIVE."
- HEATHER REYNOLDS, MA, LPC, CHT, CRRTS, LICENSED COUNSELOR AND CERTIFIED RAPID RESOLUTION THERAPY SPECIALIST

SHELBY J. FLANAGAN,

EDITOR OF THE MALSIS BOOKS WEBSITE, IS A SKILLED DANCER AND FLUTIST WITH KEEN INTUITION AND A COMPASSIONATE HEART. AT THE AGE OF EIGHT SHE STARTED USING HER CREATIVITY AND DEEP LOVE FOR HER DOG, DOLLY, TO WRITE DOLLY JEANNE THE NERVOUS SERVICE DOG. AFTER MUCH HARD WORK, SHELBY IS EXCITED TO SEE THESE DRAWINGS AT THE KITCHEN TABLE TURN INTO A REAL, PUBLISHED BOOK. "THERE WAS SOMETHING I HAD TO DO, AND I FIGURED OUT WHAT IT WAS."

LYLA T. FLANAGAN,

CONTENT CREATOR FOR DOLLY JEANNE, THE NERVOUS SERVICE DOG AND THE MALSIS BOOKS WEBSITE, LOVES WRITING, DOGS, AND ESPECIALLY CREATING STORIES INSPIRED BY THEM. THIS GRAPHIC NOVEL IS BASED ON HER OWN MALINOIS, WHO BRINGS PLENTY OF PERSONALITY AND INSPIRATION TO LYLA'S CREATIVE EXPRESSION. LYLA IS ALSO A TALENTED SINGER-SONGWRITER AND MULTIINSTRUMENTIST EXCITED ABOUT HER BRIGHT FUTURE AHEAD.

BENJAMIN WRIGHT COLEMAN,

BENJAMIN WRIGHT COLEMAN IS A DALLAS-BASED ARTIST AND ILLUSTRATOR WHOSE WORK CENTERS ON THE HUMAN FIGURE, DRAWING INFLUENCE FROM COMICS, ILLUSTRATION, AND UNDERGROUND POSTER CULTURE, COLEMAN'S WORK BLENDS SENSUALITY, AND EXISENTIAL ANGST INTO STRIKING VISUAL NARRATIVES. COLEMAN HAS DEVELOPED A CULT FOLLOWING FOR HIS COMIC-INSPIRED, ONGOING ART SUBSCRIPTION PROJECT: "HEAT DEATH", WWW.BENJAMINWRIGHTCOLEMAN.COM.

ACKNOWLEDGMENTS

FIRST AND FOREMOST, WE WOULD NOT BE PUBLISHING THIS BOOK IF NOT FOR OUR DAD, JAMES FLANAGAN. DAD, YOU BROUGHT DOLLY JEANNE INTO OUR HOME AND HAVE SELFLESSLY NURTURED AND CARED FOR HER—AND FOR US—EVERY DAY OF OUR LIVES, MOTIVATING US TO BE THE BEST WE CAN BE. YOU BELIEVE IN US, AND THAT BELIEF INSPIRED THE CREATIVITY BEHIND THIS STORY. WE LOVE YOU. THANK YOU.

WE WOULD ALSO LIKE TO THANK OUR MOM, AWARD-WINNING AUTHOR AMANDA MCKOY FLANAGAN, FOR INSPIRING US TO PUBLISH THIS BOOK AND FOR HER HELP WITH EDITING. YOU HAVE SHOWN US, BY YOUR EXAMPLE, HOW TO FINISH WHAT WE START—EVEN WHEN IT GETS HARD.

WE ARE GRATEFUL TO KEVIN T. RYAN, U.S. MARINE ARTILLERY COMBAT VETERAN AND RETIRED COLORADO ARMY NATIONAL GUARD OPERATIONS AND INTELLIGENCE NCO, FOR HIS EXPERT GUIDANCE ON THE MILITARY ASPECTS OF THIS STORY.

LASTLY, WE WANT TO THANK ALL OF THE K9S WHO KEEP US SAFE BY SERVING LAW ENFORCEMENT, OUR COUNTRY, AND CIVILIANS WITH THEIR INTELLIGENCE, AGILITY, AND KEEN SENSE OF INTUITION. YOU HUMBLY PLACE YOURSELVES IN HARM'S WAY FOR US EVERY DAY, AND WE ARE GRATEFUL FOR EACH AND EVERY ONE OF YOU.

WANT TO READ MORE?

CHECK OUT OUR WEBSITE!!
MALSISBOOKS.COM

BUY MORE ON AMAZON AND TELL YOUR FRIENDS!

JOIN OUR MAILING LIST FOR UDATES ON THE BOOK AND MORE EVENTS!

DO YOU HAVE KIDS OR DO YOU LOVE DOLLY STUFFED ANIMALS?? REACH OUT AND BUY ONE!!!

ANY QUESTIONS FEEL FREE TO EMAIL 24/7
MALSISBOOKS@GMAIL.COM

LOVED THIS BOOK?
KEEP AN EYE OUT FOR THE SECOND!

PRINCESS AT THE VATICAN

SNEAK PEEK!
DEPARTUR
FOLLOW DOLLY'S SISTER PRINCESS AS SHE EMBARKS ON THIS FAST PACED JOURNEY TO STOP A HIGHLY SOPHISTICATED INTERNATIONAL ART THEFT RING.
AS A GROUP OF THIEVES SETS IT'S SIGHTS ON THE VATICAN, PRINCESS MUST BE BRAVE AND CUNNING IN THE FACE OF DANGER IF SHE HAS ANY CHANCE AT ALL OF STOPPING THEM BEFORE IT'S TOO LATE.
PACKED WITH INTRIGUE, DANGER, AND SOME THRILLING PLOT TWISTS ALONG THE WAY, THIS IS TRULY A PAGE-TURNING ADDITION TO THE MAL SIS BOOKS SERIES.

www.ingramcontent.com/pod-product-compliance
Lightning Source LLC
LaVergne TN
LVHW070955210926
848482LV00002B/220

9798992616903